BEN 10 ALIEN FORCE™

THE GAUNTLET
&
BE-KNIGHTED

EGMONT
We bring stories to life

First published in Great Britain 2009
by Egmont UK Limited
239 Kensington High Street
London W8 6SA

Cartoon Network, the logo, BEN 10 and all related characters
and elements are trademarks of and © 2009 Cartoon Network.
(s09)
ISBN 978 1 4052 4800 6
1 3 5 7 9 10 8 6 4 2

Printed in Italy

THE GAUNTLET

Now 15 years old, Ben Tennyson has recently turned to the Omnitrix again in order to help save the world. There are some brand new awesome alien dudes for Ben to get to grips with, and some deadly villains for him to defeat. He has the help of his cousin Gwen and her magical powers. And Ben's former arch-rival, Kevin Levin, now has his own superpowers, and has joined forces with Ben and Gwen to help kick some alien tail!

Kevin is using his superpowers to fight a Techadon – a large menacing robot assassin. They're in an old disused warehouse. Kevin's body has changed to concrete, but still he's not strong enough to fight off the robot's powerful energy blasts.

Hold on! I still need a few seconds before I can change!

Gwen forms some energy shields to protect them, but the robot smashes them all.

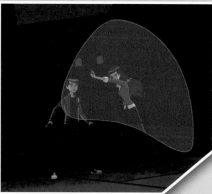

Kevin leaps up to punch the Techadon. But he grabs Kevin in his gigantic hand and squeezes his concrete shell.

Okay, I'll see what I can do.

Gwen lashes at the robot with a razor-sharp energy blast. The Techadon's hand is cut off, and Kevin plummets to the ground. The Techadon's eyes glow with anger . . .

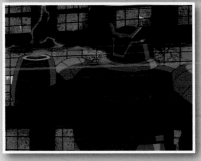

It's okay, I'm back in business. You know who'd be perfect for this?

The suspense is killing me.

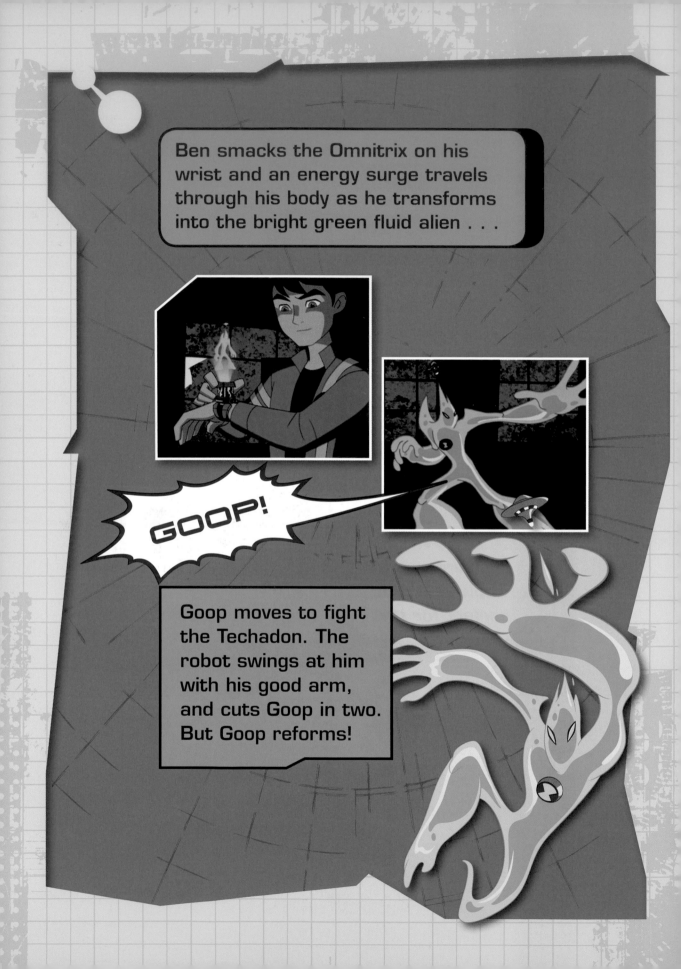

Ben smacks the Omnitrix on his wrist and an energy surge travels through his body as he transforms into the bright green fluid alien . . .

GOOP!

Goop moves to fight the Techadon. The robot swings at him with his good arm, and cuts Goop in two. But Goop reforms!

The Techadon starts firing lasers into Goop.

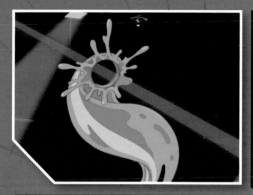

Suddenly, the Techadon fires a huge blast that sends Goop, Gwen and Kevin all flying through the wall of the warehouse.

The Techadon emerges, and Goop pushes himself into the hole where the robot's hand has started to grow back. The Techadon gradually swells and explodes.

Goop splatters all over the car park, covering Gwen and Kevin!

Yuck, Ben! Get off us!

Goop reforms and then transforms back into Ben.

Sorry! That was pretty cool, though. Like the old days.

Whatever. So long as we take care of this thing for good.

Kevin picks up the Techadon's severed hand and throws it into the boot of his car.

The next day, Kevin drives Ben and Gwen to a café. Ben walks out carrying a tray of drinks.

Nectarine smoothies for everybody!

Suddenly, someone hits the tray, and smoothies spill all over Ben.

Hey! Aw . . . I should have said **on** everybody.

Ben looks up to see two guys from his school.

Whoops. Hey, JT. Looks like somebody had an accident.

Need me to get you a sippy cup, Ben?

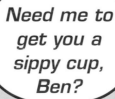

Okay, you got me. Good one.

Cash and JT laugh, and Cash gives Ben a shove. Ben's hand hovers over the Omnitrix.

You know what? You two aren't even worth it.

Huh?

That evening, Cash and JT are hungry for revenge. They spot Kevin's parked car, and decide to trash it. They push the car to the end of the road, over a cliff.

The car hits a tree stump and comes to a stop. The boot pops open and the Techadon's alien hand falls out together with a load of other alien tech. Ben, Kevin and Gwen hear the car alarm and race over.

BEEP! BEEP! BEEP!

Hey! What have you done to my car?

Grab something!

JT grabs the alien hand and he and Cash run off into the night. Ben's about to activate the Omnitrix, but changes his mind at the last minute.

Cash and JT run off to an old, abandoned mannequin factory. JT starts playing with the alien hand. Suddenly the hand shoots an energy beam up at the ceiling!

WOO HOO!

Cash grabs the hand off JT.

This'll scare Tennyson. He won't dare put me down again!

Cash blasts the lasers around the warehouse. Scared, JT runs off.

Gwen and Kevin are at the garage –
Kevin's fixing his car. JT suddenly arrives.

Where's Ben?
I gotta warn him.
Something's wrong
with Cash.

But Kevin's still angry, and forces
JT to tell him where Cash is. He
storms off to the old factory.

Kevin. Don't
do anything
stupid.

What happened to
you, JT? You and Ben
used to get on. Then
you started hanging
out with Cash.

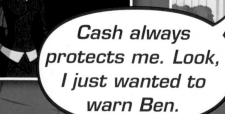

Cash always
protects me. Look,
I just wanted to
warn Ben.

Kevin arrives at the old mannequin factory, and kicks the door down.

Don't bother hiding. Your weasel friend's already told me you're here.

Cash emerges from the gloom. The alien hand has grown up his entire arm.

Pretty cool, huh? You're about to leave, right?

Kevin touches a wall and turns to concrete. He smashes the floor, making a huge hole in it.

No, this is good. Now I don't have to hold back!

Kevin takes a swipe at Cash, but Cash blocks him, and sends him flying into a wall. Blasted with lasers, Kevin collapses to the ground. He has no energy left.

Guess this means you're not the coolest kid in town anymore, Levin.

And you are? Not on your best day.

This isn't about you. This is about Ben Tennyson. You tell him, three o'clock, Mr. Smoothy car park. I'm coming for him.

Cash walks away.

Meanwhile, Gwen and JT find Ben.

There you are. I've been looking for you everywhere.

Why is he with you?

JT came to warn you.

I wasn't worried at first, but Kevin went after Cash hours ago.

You're worried about Kevin? Kevin will destroy him!

Come on, I'll show you where they are.

JT scurries off, and Ben and Gwen follow him.

Come on, let's go inside.

Inside, they find Kevin slumped against a wall.

He must have got hold of some alien tech. He looks like that robot we fought before.

Cash did this to you?

Um, when we trashed your car, we found that glove. It's possessed Cash.

Cash has challenged you to a fight, Ben. Three o'clock, at Mr. Smoothy.

Ben, Gwen and JT head away. Gwen promises to return for Kevin later.

At three o'clock, in the Mr. Smoothy car park, Cash shows up, firing laser blasts. His body is now almost completely covered in robotics, and he approaches Ben . . .

I kicked Kevin Levin's butt. And you're next, Tennyson.

Spotting JT, Cash blasts him with a laser beam. But Gwen saves him with a magic shield.

Nice friend you got there.

Cash goes to attack Gwen and JT, but Ben's transformed into . . . Chromastone!

You can't beat me, Cash.

You think just because you're some kind of freak, I'm gonna stop?

Cash laser blasts Chromastone, but the beam is deflected through his tough crystal body.

Why are you doing this? We don't win anything by fighting. Just stop.

I can't stop. This machine on me wants to fight.

That thing doesn't control you, you control it. Fight it, Cash!

Cash grimaces, then starts to glow. His metal suit slowly disappears. Just the alien glove is left on him, and JT grabs it and throws it on the ground.

Get off me!

At last, Cash is back to normal. Chromastone turns back into Ben.

Thanks for your help, Gwen.

You too, Ben. Come on, Cash. Let's go.

JT and Cash walk off.

I feel like I'm forgetting something.

You are. We must lock that robot glove up so it can't take control of anyone else.

True. But that's not it.

Meanwhile, back in the abandoned factory . . .

Hello? Anybody?

ALIEN PARTS

Take a look at Ben's 10 awesome aliens. They all have their own strengths and characteristics – some can fly, some have sharp claws or teeth, and some are just plain huge. Now's your chance to design your own cool alien. Maybe it could be a combination of some of Ben's aliens. Use the space here to draw your creation!

ALIEN SPOTTER

Can you tell which of Ben's aliens is which, from their shadows? Use lines to join each alien shadow to its correct colour image. Bonus points if you know each alien's name!

CHARACTER MATCH

Ben's superhero aliens each have their own unique powers. Use the clues and the picture shadows to identify each alien, and fill in your answers. Then, find the matching stickers and place them over the shadows. Beware – one of these guys may be an impostor!

1 He can change his body shape at will.

_ _ _ _ _ _ _ _ _

2 He can re-channel energy to emit laser beams.

_ _ _ _ _ _ _ _ _ _ _ _ _ _ _ _

3 They trade in alien technology.

_ _ _ _ _ _ _ _ _ _ _ _ _ _ _ _ _ _ _ _

4 He can easily grow in size.

_ _ _ _ _ _ _ _ _ _ _ _ _ _ _ _

Answers: 1 – Goop, 2 – Chromastone, 3 – The Forever Knights, 4 – Humungousaur.

CODE BUSTER

Ben, Gwen and Kevin have intercepted a message from the evil HighBreed Leader. The only problem is, it's written in code! Use the code breaker to help the gang work out what it says.

1 = a	7 = g	13 = m	19 = s
2 = b	8 = h	14 = n	20 = t
3 = c	9 = i	15 = o	21 = u
4 = d	10 = j	16 = p	22 = v	24 = x
5 = e	11 = k	17 = q	23 = w	25 = y
6 = f	12 = l	18 = r		26 = z

2	5	14	/	20	5	14	14	25	19	15	14	/
			/									/

13	21	19	20	/	2	5	/	3	1	21	7	8	20
				/			/						

ODD ONE OUT

Take a look at these aliens. One of them is very different from all the others. Draw a circle around the odd one out.

a   B   C

D   e   F

Answer: c is the odd one out as it's a baddy – a DNAlien. The others are all good-guy aliens.

BRAINSTORM

Brainstorm has claws, a powerful shell and a huge brain. Only two of these pictures are exactly the same. Can you spot them?

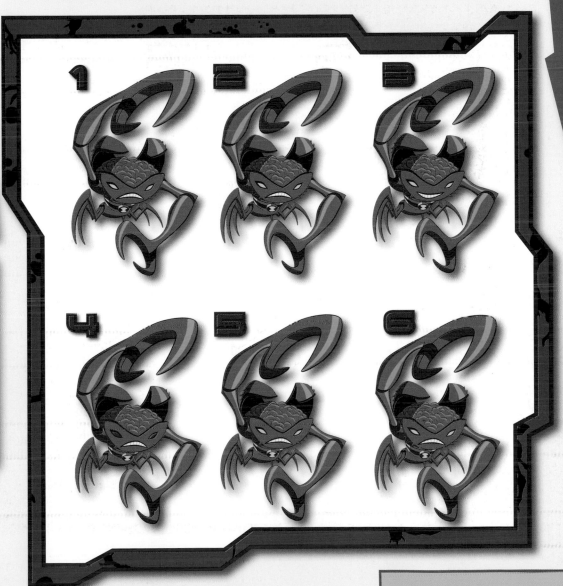

Be-KNIGHTED

The Forever Knights are human villains sworn to a secret organisation that trades in illegal alien technology. Originally formed in the Middle Ages, they now seek this alien technology for their own personal power. There's no way they can be trusted – so why is it they are looking to recruit Ben?

Inside the main hall of the Forever Knights' castle, their leader, Patrick, is standing before a large gathering of armoured Knights . . .

The Forever Knights have existed for a thousand years, with one single goal. Throughout our history we've bought, borrowed or stolen the most powerful weapons on Earth, and beyond. But so far, none has worked. This one is different.

Connor, you've earned the right to wield this quantum cannon. Aim for the heart, and hold the beam steady.

An alien weapon is handed to Connor, the bravest Knight.

The beast is chained. Don't worry.

I'll hold it steady, but how can I expect the same of the beast?

From the main hall, Connor walks through a giant door and down some stone steps to a dark chamber. There's a broken chain on the floor.

A pair of eyes glow in the darkness, and there's a low growling. Suddenly, a huge dragon emerges. It swats Connor away, races up the stone steps, and pushes against the giant door. Connor fires his weapon, but he misses, blasting a huge hole in the door instead.

The dragon breaks through the door into the main hall, and smashes through a window, flying off into the night . . .

I'll destroy you. Whatever the sacrifice, whatever the cost, I will destroy you.

Meanwhile, Ben and Gwen are hanging out, when Kevin turns up.

Ben, I've set up a meeting with the Forever Knights.

They're in trouble. They need help.

NO WAY!

Right, and that means they wouldn't be reaching out unless they have a really good reason.

Aren't you curious to find out what?

So? They're not exactly friends of ours.

He's got a point. If the Knights are desperate enough to ask me for help, we should at least hear what they have to say.

Kevin drives Ben and Gwen to the Forever Knights' castle.

They are met by a young squire.

You want me to be a part of this? Be a Knight?

A thousand years ago, some Knights battled a giant fire-breathing beast. They trapped it inside a stone fortress. The dragon is resistant to every new weapon we try on it. And now it's escaped. Ben, we need your help.

Yes, Ben. Join us in our noble cause.

Do I get some of that cool armour?

Slow down, Ben. There's still a lot we don't know.

Yeah, like if there even is a dragon?

Connor suddenly appears . . .

There certainly is a dragon. You have my word. If you have doubts, you do not belong with us.

Suddenly an alarm sounds. The group rushes inside the castle. The squire and Connor run over to a control panel, and the squire explains that they've been monitoring communications within the military.

They all watch the control panel's screen. They see a jet plane soaring through the air, with a dragon in hot pursuit. The pilot's voice comes over the air waves . . .

Target at three o'clock. It's some kind of monster. Target locked. Missiles away!

The jet fires missiles at the dragon. The angry dragon emerges from clouds of smoke.

ROARR!

The dragon blasts the jet plane with flames, and it falls from the sky. The pilot bails out with his parachute. Another plane approaches, but the dragon destroys it with fire. The dragon flies downwards . . .

You sure you don't want my help?

Ben, Gwen, Kevin, Connor and the squire all drive to the spot where the dragon is descending from the sky. They want to confront it, so they watch and wait.

Remember, all you need to do is stop it. Connor will take care of the rest.

What's it gonna be this time? Humungousaur?

Nah, Humungousaur's too close to what I'll be fighting. Gotta figure that thing's had a lot more experience being a dragon than I have!

Ben turns the Omnitrix, slams it down and transforms into a shiny, rock-hard alien . . .

CHROMASTONE!

Chromastone runs up to the dragon. The dragon blasts him with its fire – but to no effect. Chromastone releases the energy he's absorbed and throws it back at the dragon. The dragon roars and squeals.

The dragon swats Chromastone away. Chromastone gets up and hits the dragon with a concussive ray that knocks the dragon over.

Weird, but for a second there, I thought you were trying to tell me something!

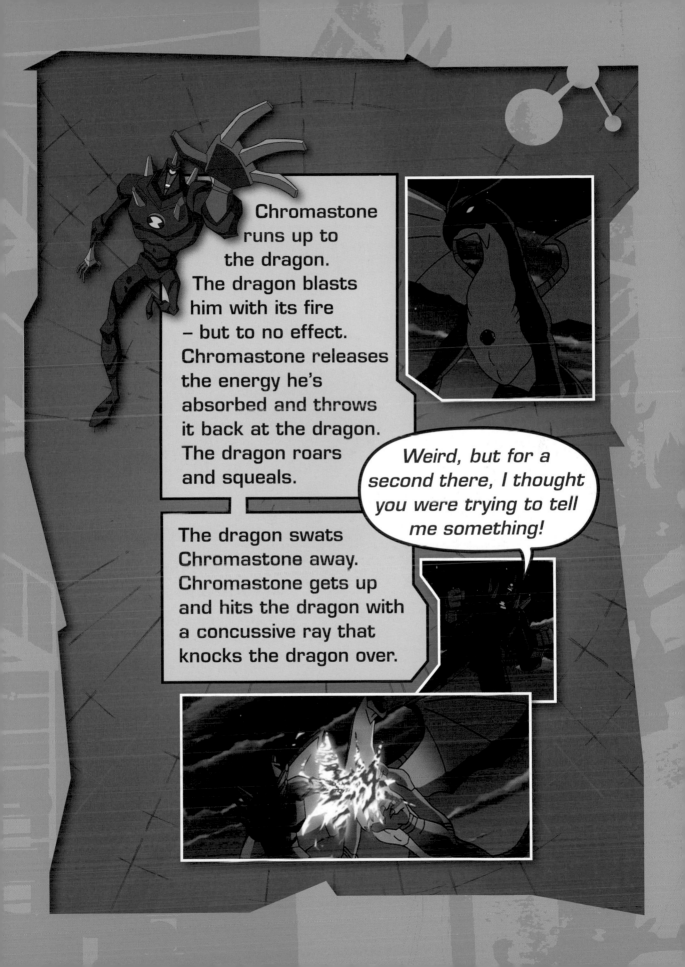

Meanwhile, Connor approaches, carrying the quantum cannon. The weapon powers up, and Connor aims it at the dragon. The squire warns him off.

Ben's too close to the dragon!

Pity.

Connor blasts the dragon, but the blast affects Chromastone, too. The ground shakes.

Connor has a warning for the squire . . .

The Knights exist for one purpose only, and you know exactly what it is.

Connor has the dragon and Chromastone still caught in the beam from his cannon. The dragon roars.

Gwen quickly fires magic laser beams towards Connor. The weapon flies out of his hands and hits the ground, shutting the beam off. The dragon flies off.

Chromastone turns back into Ben and walks over to Connor.

It wasn't personal. But if you or your friends get in my way again, it will be.

We need to have a little talk. You used me.

Ben hits the Omnitrix and turns into the huge Humungousaur. He pins Connor and the squire against their truck. The squire is spooked.

Do you know where the dragon's headed?

It's going to 6200 Prospect Boulevard. Also, the Knights found a huge relic when they caught the dragon. They've hidden it for safekeeping.

Ben, Kevin and Gwen race off in Kevin's car.

I'm telling you, when it roared there was a pattern.

So you're saying the dragon was trying to talk to you? No way.

I've got a theory. Pull over.

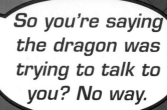

Kevin stops the car and Ben pulls out a small box from the car boot.

It's a Galvin Universo-Translator. Translates any language into any other. Pretty common alien tech.

The dragon had something like this near its throat. But it looked broken. So we need to replace the broken one with this one.

Gwen and Kevin carry on to 6200 Prospect Boulevard. Ben strikes the Omnitrix and becomes . . .

SPIDERMONKEY!

Spidermonkey grabs Kevin's translator, and scuttles into a warehouse. The powerful dragon crashes through the wall.

WHOA. Easy does it! I'm trying to help.

Spidermonkey attempts to fix the translator on to the dragon, but the roaring beast throws him off. Spidermonkey shoots out a web to hold himself up.

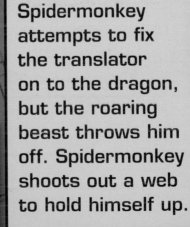

The dragon breathes fire at Spidermonkey, and he falls to the ground. Gwen forms a magic shield to protect Spidermonkey, and Kevin absorbs some concrete and throws some rubble up at the dragon. Spidermonkey takes his chance and leaps on to the dragon, fixing the translator in place. The dragon can now talk . . .

LEAVE ME ALONE.

LEAVE ME ALONE.

Spidermonkey turns back into Ben.

You can talk.

Of course I can talk. Why wouldn't I be able to?

What is it you want?

I want my ship back. My tracking signal says it's here.

The Knights are monsters. They attacked me, broke my translator box and locked me up in that dungeon.

Ship? That must be the relic the Knights have been talking about.

You're an alien, right? What were you doing here?

I was making a map of the stars. I'm a mapmaker.

Now, I want to find my ship. Then I'll head home, just as soon as those Forever Knights are destroyed.

BOOM!

Suddenly a blast blows a hole in the warehouse wall. The Forever Knights have arrived. Gwen and Kevin run outside to explain everything to Connor and the Knights. Ben stays with the dragon.

The dragon and Ben walk through the warehouse and finally find the spaceship.

The dragon touches a panel and a locker of weapons is revealed.

Ah. It's never looked better.

WEAPONS!

Didn't think I needed weapons when I landed. Too trusting.

Ben tries to talk the dragon out of using his weapons.

You don't have to do this.

But I want to. Now get out of my way.

Meanwhile, outside the warehouse . . .

He was just making a map. He wasn't going to hurt anyone. The whole thing is just kind of ridiculous, isn't it?

We have taken an oath. We live to destroy that dragon, and we will do it now!

Connor blasts the cannon at the warehouse wall. The Knights grab Gwen! Kevin absorbs some concrete, but he is blasted against the wall.

Back on the spaceship, Ben is still trying to reason with the dragon.

I've been waiting a thousand years for this.

Don't forget – you're not a monster. You're a mapmaker.

At last, the dragon listens to Ben. Outside, his spaceship suddenly crashes through the wall. Connor blasts it with his cannon, but the ship is protected by force shields. The game is up, and Connor drops his weapon and walks away. Ben heads outside.

How did you get the dragon to go?

Oh, I just used my head.

Back at the Forever Knights' castle . . .

The beast flew off, Patrick. We failed, and now there's no reason for us to exist.

But we now know there's an entire planet of dragons. How soon before they arrive, wanting revenge? The world needs the Forever Knights now more than ever!

We must stand ready to fight the dragons. And the despicable traitors who help them!

Connor and all the Knights cheer.

Patrick steps over photos of Ben, Gwen and Kevin, and in the background, the young squire hangs his head in shame.

WIN!
WIN! WIN!

YOU HAVE READ THE BOOK BUT DO YOU KNOW EVERYTHING ABOUT BEN 10? SIMPLY ANSWER THESE TWO QUESTIONS AT:

WWW.EGMONT.CO.UK/BEN-10

TO WIN A BEN 10 GOODY BAG WORTH £20 EVERY MONTH! * YOU CAN FIND THE ANSWERS IN THE BOOK, SO IF YOU GET STUCK, SIMPLY GO BACK AND CHECK.

QUESTION 1: WHAT IS THE NAME OF THE BRAVEST FOREVER KNIGHT?

QUESTION 2: WHICH ALIEN DOES BEN TRANSFORM INTO TO CONFRONT BAD BULLY CASH?

TERMS & CONDITIONS APPLY, SEE ONLINE
*THIS PROMOTION EXPIRES ON 31.12.2009